Tall, Wide, and Sharp-Eye

For Keith and Pat
—M. G.

Henry Holt and Company, Inc.
Publishers since 1866
115 West 18th Street
New York, New York 10011
Henry Holt is a registered
trademark of Henry Holt and Company, Inc.
Published in Canada by Fitzhenry & Whiteside Ltd.,
195 Allstate Parkway, Markham, Ontario L3R 4T8.

Library of Congress Cataloging-in-Publication Data
Gabler, Mirko.
Tall, Wide, and Sharp-Eye: a Czech folktale / retold by Mirko Gabler.
Summary: On his way to rescue a princess held captive
in the castle of an evil sorcerer, a Bohemian prince is helped
by three extraordinary friends.
[1. Folklore, Czech.] I. Title.
PZ8.1.G125Tal 1994 [398.21]—dc20 93-8967

ISBN 0-8050-2784-X

First Edition—1994
Printed in the United States of America
on acid-free paper. ∞
1 3 5 7 9 10 8 6 4 2

Tall, Wide, and Sharp-Eye

A CZECH FOLKTALE RETOLD BY **Mirko Gabler**

HENRY HOLT AND COMPANY / NEW YORK

There once lived an old king who had an only son. One day the king said to him, "Now that you have grown up, my boy, you must find yourself a bride! Soon you will take my place. And what kind of a king would you be without a queen?"

"But, Father," said the prince, "I don't know any girls that I like! And I hate dancing at the costume ball. How will I ever find a bride?"

The king reached into his pocket and took out a key. "Here, take this key and climb into the tower. At the very top you will find an iron door. Open it. There you will find your queen."

The prince climbed the tower. He unlocked the iron door and stepped into a room he had never seen before. Around him hung pictures of princesses in fancy gowns and elegant hairdos. But the prince looked at them all and sighed. "They look so . . . so . . . boring!" But as he turned to leave, he noticed a picture covered by a curtain.

He drew the curtain aside and saw a princess different from the others. She had sparkling eyes and the friendliest smile. "She's the one!" cried the prince. And he ran to tell his father of his choice.

"Badly you have chosen," said the king gravely. "Your bride is kept under lock and key in an evil sorcerer's castle. Many brave knights have gone to free her, and not one has returned yet. Go if you must, and may you return safely to me."

At once the prince saddled his horse and rode off to find the princess. He hadn't gone very far when he lost his way deep in a forest. It was then that he heard someone calling.

"Wait! Take us with you! You'll be glad you did." Three strangers were coming up the path.

"Who are you?" asked the prince.

"They call us Tall, Wide, and Sharp-Eye!" said the tall, skinny fellow. "I'm Tall One." And with that he began to stretch until he was as tall as the tallest pine. "Shall I fetch that nest over there?" he hollered.

"Leave the nest alone and come down, Tall One! I'll be glad to take you with me!" called the prince. Now he turned to the second fellow, who was as round as a barrel.

"They call me Wide One, sir," said the stranger. And without any warning he puffed himself up as big as a house, nearly knocking the prince off his horse.

"Oh ho!" cried the prince. "They don't call you Wide One for nothing. Come along, Wide One! I might need someone like you."

The smallest of the three strangers was a lively little gnome with a scarf over his eyes. "I'm Sharp-Eye, and I'd like to join up too!"

"Sharp-Eye?" laughed the prince. "Why, with that scarf over your eyes you can't even see the road!"

"On the contrary, sir!" said the gnome smartly. "I cover my eyes because I see too well! Even with this scarf on I can see through anything. And if I take if off and look at something sharply—*fooo!*—it catches on fire! And if it can't burn, it breaks into pieces!" And with that Sharp-Eye removed his scarf and, eyeing a tree stump, he burned it to a crisp.

"Well, I'd be a fool not to take you along," said the prince. "But tell me, Sharp-Eye . . . can you see the sorcerer's castle?"

"I see it clearly, sir. A dinner is waiting for us in the dining room!"

"But do you see the princess there?"

"She's locked up in the tower by the evil wizard's power," replied the gnome. "But not to worry! With us, you have nothing to fear!" Sharp-Eye jumped on Tall One's back and led the new friends out of the woods.

Together they traveled on. By evening they came to a dark castle. The castle was full of people but none of them moved or said a word. They had all been turned to stone.

Only the dining room was brightly lit. In the middle stood a table set with four plates. The four friends were hungry, so they sat down and helped themselves to plenty of food and drink. When they were full, they began to feel very sleepy.

Suddenly—*bang!* The door flew open and there stood the evil sorcerer.

He had three iron hoops clamped around his waist. Next to him stood the prince's chosen bride. "I know what you've come for!" shrieked the sorcerer. "Take her. But first you must guard her for three nights. If she is not with you at sunrise, you will be turned to stone!"

Then the sorcerer vanished. The prince asked the princess many questions, but she could not answer him. Determined to break the spell, the prince swore not to sleep a wink. Tall One stretched himself into a rope and wove a net across the windows. Wide One blocked the door while Sharp-Eye started a fire in the fireplace so that no one could pass through the chimney. But no sooner had they done this than they were all fast asleep.

When they awoke in the morning, the princess was gone. Sharp-Eye rushed to the window. "I can see her!" he cried. "One hundred miles from here is a forest. In that forest is an oak tree. On that oak tree is an acorn, and she is that acorn! Come, Tall One! We'll have her back in no time!"

Tall One put Sharp-Eye on his shoulders, stretched his legs, and stepped out the window. And before you could say *Istanbul* they were back, and the princess was in her chair.

And none too soon. *Bang!* The door flew open and the sorcerer rushed into the room. When he saw the princess there, he shrieked with hate. *Crack!* One iron hoop snapped away from his waist and crashed to the floor in pieces. Furious, the sorcerer disappeared, taking the princess with him.

The prince and his companions spent the day wandering through the gloomy castle. Except for a spider, not one living creature did they find. Everywhere they looked they saw nothing but figures of stone. Knights, servants, even children and their pets stood still, silent and cold to the touch.

But just as the day before, they found plenty to eat and drink in the dining room. After supper the sorcerer brought the princess for them to guard. But try as they might, they could not stay awake. And in the morning the princess was gone.

"Wake up, Sharp-Eye!" cried the prince. "Where is she now?"

"Two hundred miles from here is a mountain, sir. In that mountain is a rock. In that rock is a diamond, and she is that diamond!" Sharp-Eye climbed onto Tall One's back, Tall One stretched his legs, and jumping twenty miles a leap, he reached the mountain. There Sharp-Eye took off his scarf. He cracked the mountain open, shattered the rock that held the diamond, and grabbed the diamond. They ran back, reaching the castle just as the sky was turning pink.

When the sorcerer came and saw the princess, he was livid.

Crack! His second hoop snapped in two and the angry sorcerer led the princess away.

For the prince and his friends the day passed slowly. At last evening came and the sorcerer returned with the princess. "You have been clever! But tonight you will not be so lucky!" he wheezed, and then disappeared.

More than ever the prince and his companions tried to stay awake. They told stories, they played cards. But all in vain. One by one they dozed off, and by morning the princess was gone.

"Hurry, Sharp-Eye!" cried the prince. "Where is she now?"

"She's far, far away, sir!" replied the gnome. "Three hundred miles from here is a sea. In that sea is a shell. In that shell is a pearl, and she is that pearl. We can fetch her, but we'd better bring Wide One too!"

With Sharp-Eye on one shoulder and Wide One on the other, Tall One stretched his legs and headed for the sea. Sharp-Eye pointed to the shell, but Tall One could not reach it. The sea was just too deep.

"Wait," cried Wide One. He lay down on the beach and began to drink.

And he drank and drank until he was as big as a barn. Now the sea was low enough. Tall One grabbed the shell, and lifting his friends onto his back, he ran to the castle as fast as he could. But it wasn't fast at all—Wide One was just too heavy. Tall One had to put him down. And poor Wide One! You should have seen the lake he made. He nearly drowned in it himself.

Meanwhile in the castle the prince was pacing the room.

He could hear the roosters crowing in the village and still his companions were nowhere in sight.

Bang! The door opened and there stood the sorcerer, grinning.

"So! Where's the princess?" shrieked the sorcerer as he jumped around the room with joy. When suddenly . . .

. . . a seashell smashed in through the window. It fell to the floor and opened before the prince. From it rolled a single pearl.

In the very next instant the princess was there next to him.

It was Sharp-Eye who had thrown the shell. He had seen the wizard coming and in the nick of time he saved the day. The sorcerer's dreadful roar shook the castle walls. And *crack!* The last iron hoop snapped away from his bony waist. The sorcerer turned into a raven and flew out the broken window.

Right away, the princess regained her speech. "My name is Kate," she said and took the prince for a walk in the garden. All at once the castle was alive again. The goldfish in the fountain jumped. The children chased the cats. The cats chased the mice, and everyone was busying about as if the spell had never been.

All the knights came to thank the prince for setting them free. "Oh, don't thank me!" said the prince. "It's Tall, Wide, and Sharp-Eye you should thank!" But when he looked for them, they were nowhere to be found.

Truth be told, Tall, Wide, and Sharp-Eye didn't much care for castle life and fancy weddings. A good adventure was more to their taste. And so, seeing that their work was done, they picked up and left.

And they are wandering the world to this very day.